Sommer-Time Stories-Classics

Sommer's lively retelling of this classic Aesop fable.

ANDROCLES AND THE LION

Retold by Carl Sommer
Illustrated by Jorge Martinez

First Edition

Library of Congress Cataloging-in-Publication Data

Sommer, Carl, 1930-
  Androcles and the lion / retold by Carl Sommer ; illustrated by Jorge Martinez. -- First edition.
    pages cm. -- (Sommer-time stories-classics)
  Summary: "The slave Androcles risks his life for freedom. While in hiding, he develops an unusual friendship with an injured lion. Both Androcles and the lion are captured, and Androcles's punishment leads him to freedom"-- Provided by publisher.
  ISBN 978-1-57537-075 0 (library binding : alk. paper) -- ISBN 978-1-57537-424-6 (epub)
  ISBN 978-1-57537-474-1 (kf8) -- ISBN 978-1-57537-487-1 (pdf)
  [1. Fables.] I. Martinez, Jorge, 1951- illustrator. II. Title.
PZ8.2.S635An 2014
[E]--dc23
                              2012037797

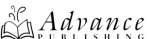

Advance
PUBLISHING

"You're not making enough bricks!" barked the angry slave master as he shook his whip in Androcles's face.

Androcles looked up and whispered, "Sir, I'm working as hard and fast as I can."

3

"You lazy worker!" yelled the furious slave master. He yanked Androcles's arm and shouted, "Come with me! I know you can work faster. You're getting whipped! I'm making you an example for the other workers."

The slave master marched Androcles to the whipping post and tied him up. As the whip slashed across Androcles's back, the slave master yelled, "This will teach you to work faster!"

Every time Androcles felt the whip, he gritted his teeth and groaned to himself, "Ohhhhh! If only I could be free!"

When the slave master untied Androcles from the whipping post, he warned, "Every day you don't make enough bricks, you're getting whipped! Do you understand?"

"Yes, sir," Androcles said softly.

The next day Androcles told another worker, "I'm so weak from my beating yesterday. But I'm going to work as fast as I can to make enough bricks. I sure don't want another beating."

"I don't blame you," the worker said.

But in spite of trying to work as hard as he could, Androcles could not make enough bricks. At the end of the day he groaned, "What can I do? I'm working as fast as I can, but I can't satisfy the slave master."

Suddenly, Androcles's face lit up. "I'll run away!"

"You can't run away," a worker reminded him. "If they catch you, they'll feed you to the starving lions."

When the slave master came and looked at Androcles's work, he yelled, "Didn't I warn you that if you didn't do what I told you, you'd be whipped?"

"Yes, sir," whispered Androcles.

That night Androcles was whipped again. Day

after day this continued. One day as Androcles lay on his straw bedding he said, "What can I do? My best is never enough, and every beating leaves me weaker than the day before. These beatings will kill me. Ohhhhh! How I wish I were free!"

Suddenly, he sat up. "Tomorrow I'm running away!" he declared. "If I get caught and fed to a hungry lion, at least I'll have my freedom for a few days."

The next day while making bricks, Androcles
watched carefully for his chance to escape. When
he was sure no one was looking, he raced into the
woods and ran until he could run no more.

Then he sat down on a rock and rested. He took
a deep breath and sighed, "At least one good thing
will happen today. Tonight I won't be whipped."

Soon Androcles became hungry. "I've got to find something to eat," he said. "I'll first make a bow and arrow and then search for food."

As Androcles searched for food, he thought, "I've got to be extremely careful that no one sees me. If anyone does, he'll report me to the emperor's soldiers. Then they'll feed me to the lions."

One day Androcles heard a strange sound. "What's that?" he asked. He tiptoed towards the sound and peeked through a bush. He froze. "A lion! I better get out of here fast."

But when he saw the lion moaning and groaning and not rushing to attack him, he said, "There must be something wrong with that lion."

When the lion saw Androcles, he held out his bleeding, swollen paw. "Oh, my!" said Androcles. "Look at that poor lion. I'll try to help him."

Slowly, Androcles went towards the lion. The giant cat purred like a kitten. When Androcles got closer, he said, "You poor thing. You have a big thorn in your paw."

Androcles knelt beside the lion. When the lion laid his paw on his lap, Androcles said with a kind voice, "Let me pull out this thorn."

Then he carefully pulled the thorn out and bandaged the paw with his extra shirt. The grateful lion licked his face as he worked. Then the lion limped along and led Androcles to his cave.

As soon as the lion felt better, he went hunting. When the lion found food, he shared it with Androcles. "I'm so thankful!" said Androcles. "Now I have something to eat and a safe place to sleep."

But one day everything changed. The lion was captured, and Androcles had to go out and search for his own food again.

Whenever Androcles had extra time, he would sit on the side of a hill and watch the townspeople. "Ohhhhh!" he often groaned. "If only I were truly free! How wonderful that would be!"

One day Androcles sneaked into the city. He watched a boy, who had many toys of his own, yank a ball from his sister. The mother saw this and scolded, "Give the ball back!"

The boy threw the ball at his sister. Then he stormed away and yelled, "Take your ball!"

Androcles shook his head and said, "Look at that selfish boy. He's mad over a silly ball. That boy needs to appreciate the many things he has."

Androcles watched men, women, and children arguing and complaining. "Don't they appreciate what they have?" he asked. "Look at them. They're free, have fine homes, nice clothes, and lots of good food. Yet they go around grumbling. How foolish they are."

One day a young man saw Androcles in the woods hunting. The man quickly went to the officials and said, "I'm sure I saw a runaway slave in the forest!"

"Quick!" the official shouted to the soldiers. "That may be Androcles, the runaway slave. We've been searching a long time for him. Put a search team together, and don't forget the dogs!"

Soldiers quickly got the dogs and mounted their horses to search for Androcles.

When Androcles heard horses and the barking
dogs, he ran behind a rock to hide. "Ohhhhh!" he
groaned. "I'm sure they'll find me now."

The mean dogs quickly surrounded him and
barked madly.

Soldiers came quickly and grabbed Androcles.
"Are you Androcles, the runaway slave?" a soldier
asked.

"Yes, I am," Androcles said.

Without another word, the soldiers tied
Androcles's hands behind his back, put him on a
horse, and took him away.

A soldier threw Androcles in jail, and yelled, "Get in there, you runaway slave. Tomorrow you'll stand before the emperor."

As Androcles stared out of his cell, he said, "No doubt I'm going to die, but at least for a short time I was a free man."

The next day the soldiers opened the cell door
and demanded, "Come with us!"

They marched Androcles to the emperor. "Are
you Androcles, the runaway slave?" the emperor
asked.

Androcles held his head high and said, "Yes,
your Majesty, I am."

"Why did you run away?" asked the emperor.

"My master had me make bricks. I worked as fast and hard as I could, but my master was never happy, so every day he whipped me."

"Don't you know the law says runaway slaves are to be fed to the hungry lions?"

"Yes, your Majesty."

"I must fulfill the law. Tomorrow you'll be fed to the lions."

The next day the stadium was crowded. One neighbor said to his friend, "This should teach runaway slaves to obey their masters."

"It sure will," the neighbor replied.

As they led Androcles out, the crowd stood and booed. When the soldiers opened the gate, a

starving lion gave a mighty roar that thundered throughout the stadium.

The crowds cheered. The lion raced toward Androcles. The lion leaped in the air, opened his mouth wide, and was ready to attack. Suddenly, the lion detected a smell!

The lion quickly turned his head and fell to the ground. He knew it was Androcles! The lion crawled towards him, purring like a kitten.

"My dear friend!" exclaimed Androcles as he put his arms around the lion. Then the lion put his paw on Androcles's lap and began licking his face.

The emperor and crowd were astonished. They had never seen anything like this before. "What is happening?" the angry emperor demanded. "Did they feed the lion before he came out?"

"No, sir," replied an official. "We are sure the lion was not fed for a week."

"This is unbelievable!" the emperor exclaimed. "Bring Androcles right away to my palace."

They brought Androcles before the emperor. "Why didn't the lion attack you?" the puzzled emperor asked.

Androcles bowed and said, "Your Majesty, I met this lion when he had a thorn in his paw. I removed the thorn and bandaged his paw with a shirt. We became best friends, and we lived together in a cave until he was captured."

"I've heard enough," the emperor said. "Give this kind man and the lion their freedom."

"Thank you! Thank you!" Androcles said as he bowed before the emperor. "I will be forever grateful for your kindness."

Androcles went to the lion's cage and led the lion to his freedom.

Androcles appreciated his freedom so much that he went throughout all the towns and villages telling everyone his story. He declared that everyone should be valued and slavery should be done away with.

At the close of every speech, he said, "Men, women, and children, always be thankful and appreciate your freedom."

Books that Motivate Children to Succeed

ISBN 978-1-57537-075-0

ISBN 978-1-57537-079-8

ISBN 978-1-57537-076-7

ISBN 978-1-57537-080-4

ISBN 978-1-57537-081-1

ISBN 978-1-57537-082-8

ISBN 978-1-57537-083-5

ISBN 978-1-57537-084-2

ISBN 978-1-57537-077-4

ISBN 978-1-57537-085-9

ISBN 978-1-57537-078-1

ISBN 978-1-57537-086-6

Sommer's Lively Retelling of These Classic Fables

- Androcles and the Lion
- The Boy Who Cried Wolf
- Chicken Little
- The Country Mouse and the City Mouse
- The Emperor's New Clothes
- The Lion and the Mouse
- The Lion and the Three Bulls
- The Little Red Hen
- Little Red Riding Hood
- The Miller, His Son, and Their Donkey
- Stone Soup
- The Tortoise and the Hare

Library Edition: Cloth Reinforced Binding 8 1/4" x 11 1/4"
Set of 12: ISBN 978-1-57537-087-3

Available In Digital Format
www.AdvancePublishing.com